MR.PERFECT

by Roger Hargreaves

It was a perfect summer's day.

And on this perfect summer's day,
Mr Perfect was looking more perfect
than usual.

He didn't have a hair out of place.

Mr Perfect lived in Tiptop Cottage.

And on this perfect summer's day,
his house was also looking even more
perfect than usual.

Not a curtain out of place.

I suppose you're wondering why
Tiptop Cottage was looking so perfect.

I shall tell you.

It was Mr Perfect's birthday,
and he was going to have a party.

There was a knock at the door.
"Perfect!" cried Mr Perfect.

"How very kind of you," he said, when he saw that all his guests had brought wonderful-looking presents.
"Please do come in, and if no one minds, we'll open the presents later."

Nobody minded in the least.

Well almost nobody.

"WHAT'S THAT?" roared Mr Uppity.

"I don't have any time to waste, you know!
You'd better make sure we
don't get bored today!"

Do you think this upset Mr Perfect?

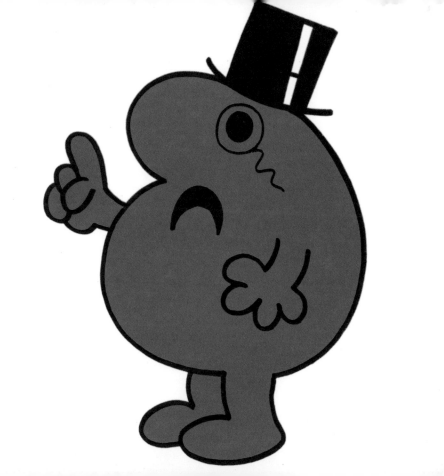

Of course not.

Mr Perfect had perfect manners,
unlike rude Mr Uppity.

"Oh no, my dear Mr Uppity,
we shan't be bored today," he replied.
"First of all we shall dance."

And everybody danced.

Even Mr Uppity.

But although he danced, Mr Uppity
couldn't manage a smile.

Unfortunately, Mr Clumsy,
being his usual clumsy self,
broke a pile of plates.

Do you think this upset Mr Perfect?

Not at all.

"Don't worry, Mr Clumsy," said Mr Perfect.

And, being the perfect person he was,
and not in the least bit clumsy,
he produced a whole lot more plates ...

... made of cardboard!

Then, he brought in a cake.

It was huge.

It looked wonderful.

It smelt terrific.

And ...

Mr Greedy thought it tasted delicious.

He gobbled up the whole cake
in three seconds flat!

There wasn't a crumb left for anybody else!

Do you think this upset Mr Perfect?

Not in the least.

Being perfect, he had already guessed
what would happen.

Quickly, he brought out lots of small cakes.

There were plenty for everybody.

Even Mr Perfect.

But as he was not greedy, he only ate one.

One cake was just perfect for him.

Once everything had been eaten,
Mr Perfect opened his presents.

He said as many thank-yous as
there were presents.

Well, not quite.

"What about my present?" cried Mr Mean.

Mr Mean's parcel was so small that
Mr Perfect had not seen it!

Mr Perfect opened the tiny parcel,
wrapped in newspaper.

"Oh, Mr Mean," said Mr Perfect.
"You've given me a lump of coal.
How kind of you!
It's delightful!"

"If I'd known, I'd only have given him
half a lump," grumbled Mr Mean.

"THAT'S IT! I've had enough!"
cried Mr Uppity, suddenly.

"I'm fed up with you, Mr Perfect. And do you
know why? I'll tell you! I have discovered
that there is a most enormous, unbearable,
exasperating fault with you."

"Would you be so kind as to tell me what
that might be?" asked Mr Perfect,
as politely as ever.

"Don't you understand?" cried Mr Uppity.
"Your fault is ...

... that you have NO faults!"

3 Great Offers for MR. MEN Fans!

MR. MEN TOKEN

1 New Mr. Men or Little Miss Library Bus Presentation Cases

A brand new stronger, roomier school bus library box, with sturdy carrying handle and stay-closed fasteners.
The full colour, wipe-clean boxes make a great home for your full collection.
They're just £5.99 inc P&P and free bookmark!

☐ MR. MEN ☐ LITTLE MISS (please tick and order overleaf)

2 Door Hangers and Posters

In every Mr. Men and Little Miss book like this one, you will find a special token. Collect 6 tokens and we will send you a brilliant Mr. Men or Little Miss poster and a Mr. Men or Little Miss double sided full colour bedroom door hanger of your choice. Simply tick your choice in the list and tape a 50p coin for your two items to this page.

PLEASE STICK YOUR 50P COIN HERE

Door Hangers (please tick)
☐ Mr. Nosey & Mr. Muddle
☐ Mr. Slow & Mr. Busy
☐ Mr. Messy & Mr. Quiet
☐ Mr. Perfect & Mr. Forgetful
☐ Little Miss Fun & Little Miss Late
☐ Little Miss Helpful & Little Miss Tidy
☐ Little Miss Busy & Little Miss Brainy
☐ Little Miss Star & Little Miss Fun

Posters (please tick)
☐ MR. MEN
☐ LITTLE MISS

3 Sixteen Beautiful Fridge Magnets – any 2 for £2.00!
inc.P&P

They're very special collector's items!
Simply tick your first and second* choices from the list below
of any 2 characters!

1st Choice
- ☐ Mr. Happy
- ☐ Mr. Lazy
- ☐ Mr. Topsy-Turvy
- ☐ Mr. Bounce
- ☐ Mr. Bump
- ☐ Mr. Small
- ☐ Mr. Snow
- ☐ Mr. Wrong
- ☐ Mr. Daydream
- ☐ Mr. Tickle
- ☐ Mr. Greedy
- ☐ Mr. Funny
- ☐ Little Miss Giggles
- ☐ Little Miss Splendid
- ☐ Little Miss Naughty
- ☐ Little Miss Sunshine

2nd Choice
- ☐ Mr. Happy
- ☐ Mr. Lazy
- ☐ Mr. Topsy-Turvy
- ☐ Mr. Bounce
- ☐ Mr. Bump
- ☐ Mr. Small
- ☐ Mr. Snow
- ☐ Mr. Wrong
- ☐ Mr. Daydream
- ☐ Mr. Tickle
- ☐ Mr. Greedy
- ☐ Mr. Funny
- ☐ Little Miss Giggles
- ☐ Little Miss Splendid
- ☐ Little Miss Naughty
- ☐ Little Miss Sunshine

*Only in case your first choice is out of stock.

— **TO BE COMPLETED BY AN ADULT** —

**To apply for any of these great offers, ask an adult to complete the coupon below and send it with
the appropriate payment and tokens, if needed, to MR. MEN CLASSIC OFFER, PO BOX 715, HORSHAM RH12 5WG**

☐ Please send ____ Mr. Men Library case(s) and/or ____ Little Miss Library case(s) at £5.99 each inc P&P

☐ Please send a poster and door hanger as selected overleaf. I enclose six tokens plus a 50p coin for P&P

☐ Please send me ____ pair(s) of Mr. Men/Little Miss fridge magnets, as selected above at £2.00 inc P&P

Fan's Name _____

Address _____

_____ **Postcode** _____

Date of Birth _____

Name of Parent/Guardian _____

Total amount enclosed £ _____

☐ **I enclose a cheque/postal order payable to Egmont Books Limited**

☐ **Please charge my MasterCard/Visa/Amex/Switch or Delta account** (delete as appropriate)

Card Number

Expiry date __/__ **Signature** _____

Please allow 28 days for delivery. Offer is only available while stocks last. We reserve the right to change the terms
of this offer at any time and we offer a 14 day money back guarantee. This does not affect your statutory rights.
Data Protection Act: If you do not wish to receive other similar offers from us or companies we recommend, please
tick this box ☐. Offers apply to UK only.

MR.MEN   LITTLE MISS
Mr. Men and Little Miss™ & ©Mrs. Roger Hargreaves

CUT ALONG DOTTED LINE AND RETURN THIS WHOLE PAGE